Forbidden Love

Forbidden Love

Iridescent Toad Publishing

Iridescent Toad Publishing.

Cover design by Annie Hara.

First edition. ISBN: 978-1-913779-05-4

Chapter One

Daylight blanketed the little kingdom in a gentle and promising glow. Amongst a palace and many smaller buildings, at the very end of a long, cobbled path, was an old château. No amount of sunlight could soften the sorrow that loomed over one of its residents. For within the foreboding walls of the château, was Cinderella, afraid and lonely.

The building had been in her family for generations, previously in her father's name. During his lifetime, he was always kind to Cinderella. She had never been left wanting for anything; she had enjoyed being able to wear the nicest clothes, and often the pleasure of dining on the finest foods. Regardless of the gifts that her father had proudly given to her though, it was always the time with him that she had cherished the most. He had always been a thoughtful and patient man who had made time for his daughter. When his wife passed away, he ensured to be there for Cinderella in her grief at having lost her mother. Just a young girl at the time, Cinderella missed her mother terribly.

Cinderella's father was a valiant man who cared deeply for his daughter's happiness. So much so that in thinking that she was in need of a female figure in her life, he remarried one Lady Sharp. When the woman became Cinderella's stepmother, it gave Cinderella two stepsisters: Holly and Charlotte.

Cinderella had always thought of her stepmother as being Sharp by name, sharp by nature. They had never truly got on well with each other. The situation hadn't been too bad at first but when Cinderella's father passed away, it soon became apparent that things were about to go from bad to worse.

With Cinderella's only remaining blood relative out of the picture, Lady Sharp, Holly and Charlotte were absolutely awful towards her. They had always been cold towards her but without her father around, they took their volatility to another level.

Outnumbered by the sheer power of female jealousy and passive aggression, Cinderella was forced to become a slave in her own home. If not for the friends that she had nearby, things could have been even worse for her.

****

Having drifted in and out of a restless slumber as the hessian of her bedding had done little to comfort her, Cinderella slowly awoke to the sound of a distinctly rhythmic knock at the door. From that alone, she knew who would be there and waiting to see her.

Peeking through the strands of her tousled hair, she sat up enthusiastically. She was looking forward to seeing her friends – Max, Phillip and Claire. The three of them were employees of the kingdom, recruited to run errands and pass on messages. Like Cinderella, they were all in their early twenties. She had a better rapport with them than with her stepfamily. Although she didn't get much chance to socialise outside of her home, she was always grateful for the small moments each day where she could see Max, Phillip and Claire. Quietly aware of their friend's situation, they were always keen to catch up with her.

Cinderella quickly bundled her bedding up into a ball and threw it across the room as she promptly stood up. Rushing to tie her apron around her dress and quickly tying her hair into a messy ponytail, she was bursting to answer the door before anyone else could. Creeping downstairs as stealthily as possible, she was relieved to notice that the three other women in the château were still asleep. It meant that she would be able to get to the door in time to see her friends.

"It's a beautiful day, Cinderella," said Claire. "There's not a single cloud in the sky. Once I've got all the deliveries done, I'm going to sit outside and enjoy it."

Cinderella noticed that her friend's delivery bag was full of envelopes. It was in better condition than both of their ragged clothes – it had to be in order to take the weight of everything inside it. Although Claire worked hard and didn't have much to show for it, as she maintained a firm grip on the weight of the delivery bag, she had a smile that beamed across her pretty face from ear to ear.

"It looks like a gorgeous day," Cinderella agreed as she observed the sunlight coming into the hallway from outside.

"It's a busy one for us today," Max said as he handed her an elaborately decorated piece of paper.

"Not that we're not happy to stop by and say hello," said Phillip.

"We wish we could stay and chat for a bit longer," added Claire. "But there has been so much going on."

"Oh?" Cinderella verbalised curiously. "What is it? What's…"

She was suddenly interrupted by the sound of an intolerable screech coming from somewhere within the château. Claire looked at her sympathetically.

They all knew who the voice belonged to.

"I'd better go," said Cinderella. "Stepmother is shouting for me."

Cinderella's friends smiled awkwardly. They all knew that she would be in trouble for simply having opened the door to say good morning. Before closing it, she gestured to them that she would be back. Then, still with the piece of paper in her hand that Max had given to her, she darted up the stairs to see what Lady Sharp wanted. Knowing already that it would be something trivial, Cinderella knocked cautiously on the tall grand door of her stepmother's bedroom. When she heard no response, she crept into the darkness of the room. She was used to having to work hard for even a simple interaction with the woman. She could just about see Lady Sharp's cat, Tiffany.

Upon closer inspection, she could tell that on the bed next to the demure creature, was the ungrateful woman.

"Ugh!" she groaned in a bitter tone. "You took your time, Cinderella."

Tapping her tail on the luxurious duvet mischievously, Tiffany almost looked just as dissatisfied as her owner.

"Sorry," said Cinderella as she timidly passed the piece of paper in her hand to her stepmother.

As Lady Sharp moved to open the curtains in order to read the letter, Cinderella instinctively took a step back. The woman's presence was always overbearing.

"Holly! Charlotte! Get in here," Lady Sharp called loudly.

Before she knew what was happening, Cinderella found herself being shoved out of the way by her two stepsisters. In no time at all they were at their mother's side, listening intently as she read the letter with clear, well-spoken diction.

"You are all invited to a ball at the palace tonight. Every maiden in the kingdom is to attend. Please dress well and prepare to meet the Prince, who – albeit cautiously – is looking for love."

"That's so exciting," Holly enthused as she snatched the paper away from Lady Sharp. "I would love to marry a prince."

"Too bad," said Charlotte. "Why would he want to marry you, when he could have me? I'm sure he'd choose me over you any day."

As the two sisters started to indulge in one of their trademark squabbles, Lady Sharp forcefully moved to stand in between them.

"Enough!" she commanded. "You both need to think about what you are going to wear to the ball."

"Can I come too?" Cinderella asked, almost pleadingly.

Usually, she wouldn't dare to ask but, as far as she could recall, nobody in the kingdom – outside of the royal circle – had ever been invited to a ball at the palace before. It wasn't the thought of the Prince that piqued her interest though; she just wanted the opportunity to go somewhere different, and to wear something nice for a change.

"What use would you be at a ball?" Charlotte

asked, a sadistic smirk widening across her face.

"Yeah," Holly added, laughing and keen to mock Cinderella further. "She's not going, is she, Mother?"

"It says that all maidens are invited," Cinderella said anxiously. "I'm a maiden, so that means that I'm invited too."

"Ok," said Lady Sharp, her eyes narrowing wickedly. "You can go."

Cinderella was so relieved by the answer that she almost managed to ignore the sound of her stepsisters shouting in protest.

"Don't assume anything, girls," said Lady Sharp. "Cinderella can go to the ball, but only if she gets everything done here. That includes helping the three of us to get ready for it."

"Good," Charlotte said. "I need her to do some sewing."

"Don't forget me," insisted Holly. "I need a lot of ironing done."

Cinderella wasn't at all surprised by the demands that Holly and Charlotte were making. It quickly dawned on her that she was going to have a hectic day ahead. Although she felt sad that she wouldn't have much time to get herself ready for the ball, she promised herself that she would stay positive. There was still a lot to look forward to. Remembering to stay humble as required, she thanked Lady Sharp before leaving the room.

Cinderella soon found herself stood on the landing, waiting on Holly and Charlotte as they shouted to her from inside their respective bedrooms. They had plenty of dresses to choose from and ungratefully, they spent a lot of time throwing them into Cinderella's arms whilst going through their wardrobes. In contrast, Cinderella knew that her only option was a dress that her mother had left to her. She didn't mind at all that it was old-fashioned – not only did it have sentimental value, but it was beautifully distinctive.

Finally, she was able to get back to the front door. She was grateful that her friends had waited a good while for her by that point. They had done a few more errands before coming back to sit patiently on the grass. They had a feeling that she would need them on this occasion, and they weren't wrong.

Ushering Max, Phillip and Claire inside the château as discretely as she could, Cinderella led them up to her room and quickly told them what was going on.

"You don't have much time to get everything done," Max said, a concerned frown on his face.

"I agree that my chances are probably quite slim," said Cinderella as she motioned towards the noise coming from her stepfamily. "As long as we can do something to make this dress look as good as possible though, it should all be ok."

"You can do this," Claire said kindly as she gave Cinderella a hug. "We'll help you."

"You never know what good things could happen at the ball," Phillip said, smiling suggestively.

They all knew that he wasn't hinting at anything crass, not at all. In fact, it was clear to all of them that deep down, Cinderella would do anything for a golden ticket to get her away from her horrible stepfamily.

"You can all read me like a book," Cinderella said with a soft sigh.

"Chin up, Cinds," Max said as he patted her on the shoulder. "You'll get to the ball and it will be amazing. Just you wait and see."

Just as they had needed to do many times before, Cinderella's friends crept out of the château. Left to her own devices, she meticulously worked through all of her tasks. She managed to get every dress ready apart from her own. She was keen to get things right, and more so due to the anxious feeling that her chances of going to the ball were temperamental at best. She sighed, wishing so hard that she could be somewhere else.

Chapter Two

Things were looking doubtful. It had taken Cinderella so long to help her stepsisters get ready that there were still jobs to do around the château. *I'll never manage to get everything finished and get myself ready for the ball*, she thought sadly as she finished scrubbing the kitchen floor.

Although there was still much to do, she quickly darted upstairs towards her room. She needed a moment to herself, just to get her head together. When she opened the door, she was met with a pleasant surprise. Max, Phillip and Claire were standing in the corner of the room – and next to them was the dress that Cinderella hoped to wear to the ball. It was draped elegantly on a hanger against the wardrobe door. Cinderella was delighted to notice that it had been ironed and that extra diamantes had been added. Shocked at what her friends had done for her, she was speechless.

"We hope you like it," Claire said sweetly, happy

to break the silence. "We were a bit nervous about customising it, what with the sentimental value it has to you. We took a bit of a risk in deciding to go ahead with it – we want you to look your best and to have a great time at the ball."

"I can't believe you all managed to sneak in here without being noticed," said Cinderella, still dumbfounded. "Were you afraid of getting caught?"

"No," said Max. "If one of those horrible women had caught us, we'd have just charged out of here. I can't imagine that they'd be able to run very fast, even if they wanted to."

Cinderella giggled at the thought of her stepmother and stepsisters haplessly trying to run.

"We didn't finish all of our deliveries today," said Phillip. "To be honest though, we're willing to take the risk of getting into trouble over it, on this occasion anyway. Right now, it's important to us to be able to help you."

Feeling as if she was about to cry, Cinderella quickly lunged forwards to hug her friends. The love and care that they had shown towards her touched a nerve, and all the more so because it was in such stark contrast to how her stepfamily treated her.

Cinderella was starting to believe that she really would be going to the ball. It dawned on her that all she needed to do to get ready was to put the dress on. She had never been one for wearing makeup and besides, she had good skin.

Reaching his hand into his pocket, Max took out a necklace.

"It's probably best that you don't ask me where I got this from," he said cheekily. "But just know that I did it for you."

Cinderella gave him a warm smile. She knew that her friends hadn't had an easy life and that they were used to having to beg, steel or borrow to get by. She couldn't be mad at them.

Claire put the necklace around Cinderella's neck and helped her to get into the dress. For the first time in a long time, Cinderella felt pretty. The material of the dress hugged her figure and it had a sheen to it that was almost iridescent. It was worlds apart from what she had grown used to wearing. Since the day of her father's passing, she had only ever been allowed to wear rags. Lady Sharp had taken great delight in giving them to her.

Upon hearing her stepmother and stepsisters calling to her from downstairs, Cinderella's focus was snatched away from her daydream. As she charged down the stairs to see what her stepfamily wanted, she was surprised to see that all three women were already dressed for the ball. She was sure that she had already heard them laughing and joking about leaving without her. The three of them were all dressed so elegantly. They were all too sour-faced to look truly beautiful though.

Cinderella walked carefully down the remaining steps of the staircase, holding the lower half of her dress up a little to ensure that the length of it wouldn't drag along the floor.

"Well, look at you," Holly said mockingly.

"Who does she think she is?" said Charlotte.

"Now, girls," said Lady Sharp. "Cinderella has completed her chores. We had an agreement that upon doing so, she could go to the ball. I am a woman of my word, am I not?"

Nobody wanted to answer Lady Sharp's question. Besides, in that moment, she didn't look particularly committed to what she was saying anyway.

Although the interaction with her stepfamily was making her incredibly nervous, Cinderella was still hopeful that they would now all be able to head off to the ball together. She still didn't know what to say and so smiled sheepishly, simply hoping for the best. She shyly made eye contact with one of her stepsisters, but soon wished that she hadn't.

"She's wearing my necklace!" Holly complained indignantly. "Give it back!"

Before Cinderella could do anything to defend herself, Holly was clawing at her. In mere moments, the necklace was ripped away from Cinderella's neck. Most of the beads bounced on the floor, each pretty colour making a delicate noise in the process.

Charlotte was keen to support her sister's unpleasant approach. She shoved Cinderella against the wall and then emptied the glass of red wine that she had been nursing all over her stepsister's dress. In a final surge of aggression, Charlotte grabbed at the dress and yanked it so hard that the distinctive sound of fabric tearing caused everyone in the room to fall silent.

"That's enough, girls," Lady Sharp announced nonchalantly. "We need to get going now. We don't want to be late."

With that, Holly and Charlotte charged out of the front door. Before following along behind them, Lady Sharp turned to lock it, smirking sadistically at the broken young woman.

"We'll see you when we get back," she said coldly.

Alone in her ruined dress and still able to see some of the beads from the broken necklace on the floor, Cinderella slid down against the wall. With her head in her hands, she began to sob. Hard, gulping, pain-tainted sobs. She needed to get away. She had no idea where she could go, but she didn't care as long as it would be to somewhere else.

In a blind state of sorrow, she darted through the kitchen and out of the back door of the château. She kept running until she could feel the softness of the grass beneath the soles of her feet. Having entered the large communal garden situated behind the back of the château, she continued to run until she came to a stone bench. She sat down on it, still in tears. Although she didn't know quite where she was, she felt so upset, that a part of her didn't care.

As she managed to steady her breathing, she told herself that maybe going to a ball at the palace – of all places – just wasn't for her after all. She had felt like an outcast for such a long time and maybe this was just the universe's way of telling her not to dream too big; to stay humble and, dare she admit it, realistic.

She was so deeply entrenched in her own thoughts that she didn't seem to notice when an old woman sat down on the bench next to her.

"Goodness dear, whatever is the matter?" said the woman, a kindness in her tone. "There, there. Shh… Please don't cry."

The woman's demeanour, patient and unassuming, made it easy for Cinderella to trust her. It wasn't long before she had told her everything. In her darkest moment and in feeling so desperately alone, she found it easy to be candid.

"I am disgusted to hear of how horribly they treat you," said the woman. "What bitter, unpleasant people."

It was comforting to Cinderella to know that somebody who seemed older and wiser was taking an interest in the situation.

"Listen," said the woman. "I can get you to the ball. Let me organise a carriage for you. I know it's a bit last-minute but that shouldn't be too much of a problem. Many of the commercial horse and carriage services will have already been booked by other people in the kingdom for the ball tonight. Luckily for you though, I've got my own horses in the stable nearby. They're beautiful creatures and I promise that they're up to the job."

"That's so kind," Cinderella said gratefully.

"My coachmen and footman aren't doing much tonight anyway," said the old lady. "I was hoping that they would stay in and play cards with me. They don't work for anyone else and I don't go out very often myself. Still though, as you can probably tell from me being out here tonight, we all got a bit bored indoors. It will be nice for them to take the horses out. And more importantly, it would be a pleasure to help you."

Trying to take it all in, Cinderella suddenly remembered something.

"I really appreciate your offer," she said. "I've got nothing to wear now though. My dress is ruined. I'm used to looking tatty but even I couldn't go out looking like this."

"You don't seem to think much of yourself," the old woman said with a sigh. "That's sad."

Cinderella nodded. The woman had managed to touch a nerve.

The old woman suddenly clapped her hands together and stood up enthusiastically.

"Here's an idea," she said. "I'll get Francis to have a rummage around in the wardrobe in my bedroom before he comes here with the horses. Even if he brings just a few dresses with him, I know there will be something suitable for you. And slippers: you'll need those too. I've got just the pair in mind, and I think they will look lovely on you. No matter which dress you choose to wear, they will be a good match."

"Wow!" said Cinderella, stunned and enchanted.

"Right," said the woman. "Give me forty minutes. It shouldn't take me any longer than that. I'll get the carriage to pick you up at the side gate of the garden."

Cinderella still couldn't believe what was happening.

"Here," the woman continued as she removed her shawl and passed it to Cinderella. "You can borrow this while you wait. It's getting a little cold out here. All I ask is that you're ready to be picked up from the ball at midnight. We'll meet you at the steps at the bottom of the palace. It's really important that you are no later than that – I've got a doctor's appointment in the morning."

Although Cinderella wanted to ask the lady why she was being so helpful, she didn't want to seem ungrateful or suspicious. She didn't want to miss her chance to go to the ball and so she decided to just go along with everything.

"I was like you once," said the woman. "It's a cruel world out there and it matters to be kind wherever possible. Some people never manage to do it. That's just their way. I absolutely believe that there are many people with good hearts though. You're clearly one of them and I want you to be happy. You deserve to go to the ball as much as any other maiden in the kingdom."

Before Cinderella could express her gratitude, the woman was already storming determinedly down the path. She had a generosity about her that instinctively, Cinderella trusted. She didn't know whether to be more taken aback by the woman, or by the fact that – as much as she barely dared to believe it – she would be going to the ball.

Chapter Three

The palace was so cavernous that it wasn't long before Cinderella realised that she was lost. The ball had started a good while ago and so the chances of her being able to find another reveller to show her the way were slim. The grandly-decorated walls didn't feature anything that resembled directions. She was beginning to fear that she was in the wrong part of the palace entirely and could be accused of having broken in.

Of all the places that one could get lost in, the palace wasn't the worst by any means. It was elaborately adorned in rich colours, outlined in accents of gold. Not only that, but there were paintings on the walls. They were large in size and were flattering to the appearance of those who featured in them. As Cinderella's footsteps across the marble flooring echoed on the high ceilings, she assumed that the paintings must be of royalty. She wondered to herself who else was in the royal family. Although many of the maidens at the ball were probably just there to meet the Prince, she was more excited to embrace the opportunity of being somewhere different and to meet new people.

As she turned a corner at the end of a large hallway, Cinderella was suddenly met with the anxiety of seeing a large crowd of people up ahead. They were draped in the finest of materials and they all moved around with an air of glamour and confidence. As she walked reluctantly closer towards the crowd, she noticed that there was one man in particular who all of the women seemed to be flocking around. As he stood there in his white suit greeting people politely, he seemed charming, but in many ways, disinterested. Cinderella suspected that it would be overwhelming for anyone, even a prince, to be given so much attention.

Keen to avoid the hustle and bustle of the overbearing crowd, Cinderella stood up as tall as she could, hoping to see beyond what was going on immediately in front of her. She noticed that the King and the Duke were looking on cautiously and that next to them, were several other princes and princesses. Some of them looked thrilled to be there and excited to lap up the attention, whereas others appeared to be uncomfortable about the whole thing.

Cinderella also noticed that across from the King and the Duke, there was a woman sitting on a smaller throne. She looked unhappy. Her gaze was directed towards the ground and every so often in between fiddling with the material on her ball gown, she chewed on the tips of her fingers. Despite looking lovely in her attire, with her long hair cascading down her elegant shoulders and décolleté, the woman seemed desperately uncomfortable and as if she would rather be somewhere else.

Cinderella couldn't help but stare at the woman, mesmerised by her beauty. Although it seemed as if she didn't want to be seen, to Cinderella, it was as if the woman was the only other person in the room. It impressed Cinderella that even though the woman was royalty, she appeared to have a depth to her that went beyond the obvious; she was someone who didn't need to put on a front, and someone who didn't need to be seen.

Without giving it much thought and without necessarily meaning to, Cinderella caught the gaze of the intriguing woman. She felt a blush begin to rise on her cheeks, hating the thought that she might have made the woman feel even more uncomfortable during what was already an awkward appearance for her.

Surely I am mistaken? Cinderella thought as she tried to duck behind a crowd of other guests. *She must have been looking somewhere else. Surely she couldn't have been looking at me?*

Knowing that she was now out of the woman's line of sight, Cinderella breathed a sigh of relief. As the crowd that she was hiding behind naturally ebbed and flowed away to another part of the ballroom though, she once again felt the heat rise in her cheeks. This time, she noticed that not only was the woman looking at her – she was *smiling* at her.

Enchanted by the woman, Cinderella felt an overwhelming urge to go and talk to her. She stopped herself though. *How on earth would a mere servant like me have anything of interest to say to a beautiful woman like her?* she thought.

Luckily for Cinderella, the woman motioned across to the King, as if asking him for permission to walk the room. If Cinderella had read the King's expression correctly, he seemed relieved that the woman was finally interested in engaging with the guests.

Everyone had probably been expecting the woman to remain on her throne throughout the rest of the evening. So much so that when she walked down the small series of steps that separated her throne from the dance floor, the nearby guests parted. As she continued to walk through the parting crowd, it became clear that she was heading directly towards Cinderella, who was stood like a deer who had just spotted a hunter. It wasn't long before Cinderella found herself lost for words as the woman offered her a gloved hand.

"Dance with me," said the woman.

There was something commanding in her voice that made it impossible for Cinderella to protest. More than that though, the woman's voice was calming and reassuring. As someone who was so used to being shouted at, that too took Cinderella by surprise.

Too charmed to refuse, and too stunned to speak, in just moments, Cinderella found herself being led by the woman into the centre of the ballroom. In a blur of intrigue, she was soon being led around the dance floor with the woman's hand on her lower back, guiding her along to the music of the string quartet.

"You're a good dancer," said the woman.

"I've always loved music," said Cinderella. "I often find myself dancing when doing the housework."

The woman smiled warmly at her as the King motioned to the orchestra to keep playing the waltz that echoed melodically around the room.

"I've had lessons," said the woman, nodding her head in the direction of the King. "He hired a good teacher for me when I was younger."

"Are you a princess?" Cinderella asked the woman.

"Yes," she replied with a shy smile.

As soon as the musicians finished playing their waltz and quickly started on a different piece, the Princess took that as her cue to leave the dance floor. She once again led Cinderella by the hand, this time to the edge of the ballroom.

"I don't want to be in the spotlight," she said. "The whole point of this ball is for my brother to find an eligible maiden."

Cinderella laughed, amused at how neither of them seemed interested in that aspect of the ball.

"Come for a walk with me," said the Princess. "It'll be nice to step out of here and get some fresh air."

"Won't your family mind?" Cinderella asked.

"Not at all. They know what they're doing and it doesn't really apply to me."

The further the two women walked away from the ballroom, the quieter everything became. The Princess motioned at a pair of guards in the hallway to let them past. Cinderella was in awe of how casually the Princess spoke to the guards. *This is all just normal to her*, Cinderella thought.

Once they were alone and at the end of the hallway, the Princess took the opportunity to introduce herself properly.

"I'm Arial," she said as she gave Cinderella's hand a tight squeeze.

"It's lovely to meet you," said Cinderella.

Instinctively, and without really giving it much thought, she performed a small curtsy to the adorable woman in front of her. This time, it was Arial's turn to blush. Cinderella nervously bit her lip as it dawned on her that the Princess probably didn't want to be addressed as royalty.

Although she didn't allow herself to do so, Cinderella wanted to wrap her arms around Arial in a comforting embrace. Even though they barely knew each other, there was something about Arial's energy that made Cinderella feel safe and cared about. In contrast to what she was so used to at home, the way that Arial had treated her in such a short space of time stood out and mattered to her a great deal. It was nice to be made to feel that she was wanted; that she was worth something.

Hearing Arial say something complementary about her dress, Cinderella was grateful to be distracted from her thoughts.

"Thank you," Cinderella said humbly. "It belongs to a good friend. I'll have to give it back after the ball."

As she thought about how she was wearing a borrowed dress, it reminded Cinderella that she shouldn't say too much to Arial. She figured that the Princess wouldn't want to hear about the problems at home, and the whys and wherefores behind how she eventually managed to get to the ball. Cinderella was used to being at the mercy of other people when it came to wanting to have nice things but she didn't feel that Arial – who she already admired – would want to hear about the mess that was her home life.

"It looks incredible on you," said Arial. "You look beautiful."

Arial's eyes sparkled as she looked at Cinderella. Cinderella smiled shyly, still barely able to believe that she was being given the time of day by, of all people, a princess.

"Father told me that my dress was a bold choice for the ball," said Arial. "I insisted on wearing it anyway."

She winked playfully at Cinderella, who was thrilled to observe her rebellious nature.

It must be wonderful to be your own person, and to not live in fear of offending your family, Cinderella mused. There was something about Arial that made her want to be stronger in herself – more confident and less afraid. The woman was empowered and lovely to be around. It made Cinderella wish that she could stay in the moment with Arial forever. She just had an alluring energy, and for the first time in a very long time, Cinderella felt inspired.

Chapter Four

The garden outside of the palace was spacious and well cared for. The grass was lush and the variety of tall trees provided an abundance of textures and colours. There were many different plants and flowers – more than Cinderella could name. It was a clear night and even under the moonlight alone, the beauty of the garden was impossible to miss.

The weather was perfect for a late-night stroll. Arial spoke about her life, whilst Cinderella listened attentively. She didn't hold back on any details. From her favourite flowers to her deepest spiritual beliefs, Arial felt that she could talk to Cinderella. So much so that it was easy for the two of them to forget that they were from completely different worlds.

"What's it like being a princess?" Cinderella asked.

Arial paused in thought, unsure of how to describe her lifestyle with just a simple answer.

"Hmm…" she mused, deep in thought. "It's ok, I suppose. I have never had to go without anything and truthfully, I'm used to getting my own way. It's not necessarily all it's cracked up to be though. I am respected and admired for *what* I am, but when it comes to having someone to talk to – someone who can see me for *who* I am – admittedly, it can get a bit lonely."

"Really?" asked Cinderella, shocked at Arial's answer.

"Of course," replied Arial. "I mean, I can't come and go as I please. Outside of the palace, I have to be escorted by guards at all times. It's nice that there are many things that I don't have to worry about, but there are definitely times where I have wondered how nice it might be to have a normal life."

"Wow," said Cinderella, mesmerised by Arial's candour.

It surprised Cinderella that Arial's life came with a number of restrictions. On the surface, being a Princess appeared to be fun and liberating. When getting right down to the details of it though, there were many things about the royal lifestyle that seemed stifling.

"Are your family strict with you?" Cinderella asked.

"They can be. It's nothing bad. Father just wants the best for us," Arial said, suddenly raising an eyebrow and seeming doubtful. "There are times when he worries too much though. He is probably anxious that our image would be tainted if we failed to adhere to the kingdom's expectations of us."

Arial brushed her delicate fingers over the surface of a large tree branch. She then stood up tall, putting her face up close to one of its flowers and breathing in the powdery scent. Cinderella couldn't help but watch her.

"Do you think your brother is having fun in there?" Cinderella asked as she motioned towards the palace. "He seemed a bit overwhelmed."

"I think the people of the kingdom are more excited about the ball than he is," Arial said, slightly amused. "It's no secret that my father organised it in hopes of being able to match my brother up with a maiden. I think it's because my father wants to see his grandchildren born before he passes on."

"That's understandable," said Cinderella. "What

about you? Does he want you to get married?"

"I don't think he's as concerned about whether or not I get married," said Arial, a sudden sadness in her voice. "It's so rare that I get any time and space to myself – I can't imagine that I would ever meet anybody to get married to!"

Arial's frustration was one that Cinderella could relate to. It seemed that they were both at the mercy of having to seek permission and approval from their respective families for all kinds of things. She had already resigned herself to the idea that her place in the world was to serve her stepmother and stepsisters.

"I'm glad to have met you," said Arial, an endearing honesty in her tone. "I have never met anybody who I can talk to so easily before. I'm glad for the ball, even though admittedly, I really didn't want to go."

"I could tell that you felt uncomfortable in there," said Cinderella. "You didn't look too happy when you were sat on your throne."

The two women made eye contact with each other. In the sudden pause in their conversation, there was a mutual understanding between them that spoke more than any words possibly could.

"I hope you don't mind me saying so," said Cinderella. "But you remind me of a flower."

"Oh? How so?"

"Well, you're delicate and there's so much beauty in that, but equally, *your beauty* comes from a place of strength. You strike me as someone who has weathered a few storms even though on the surface, the first thing people probably see is your physical beauty."

"That's a lovely thing to say. Thank you."

The fact that Cinderella wasn't afraid to give such a bold complement struck a chord with Arial, who was keen to return it in the spirit of being kind and being open.

"Ok. My turn," Arial said with a warm smile. "You remind me of a star. No matter how dark the night sky may be, you shine. You always shine, and brightly so."

Cinderella wasn't used to being complemented. Unsure of how to take it, she looked up at the sky.

"See," said Arial as she noticed the radiance in Cinderella's eyes. "Always shining."

There was so much more that they both wanted to say to each other but neither of them wanted to spoil the moment. Cinderella felt that by not telling Arial about her home life, she was hiding something from her. Equally though, she didn't want to burden her.

"I'm glad to be out here with you," said Cinderella. "I had to move Heaven and Earth to be able to get here tonight."

Despite Cinderella's silence on the subject, Arial already had a feeling that her life had not been an easy one.

"Tell me," Arial said calmly.

Despite how she had been careful to keep quiet about her circumstances, Cinderella didn't want to keep anything hidden from Arial, who was keen to know only out of care and concern.

"I live with my stepfamily. They can be very difficult," said Cinderella, trying not to elaborate too much through fear that it would alienate Arial. "They weren't too keen on the idea of me being here tonight."

"Did they try to stop you from attending?" Arial asked, intelligently reading between the lines as she gave Cinderella's hand a squeeze in hers.

"I don't think they like me," said Cinderella.

It made Cinderella sad to say that out loud because it made a very painful truth seem all too real. When they were children, she had been excited to think that maybe Holly and Charlotte could be friends with her. She had asked them if they would like to play with her dolls and it wasn't long before they took great delight in breaking them. Soon the dolls' blinking eyes were poked back into their plastic heads whilst their limbs were torn from their soft bodies. Despite how upset this made Cinderella, her father told her that everything would be ok and that it would take time for Holly and Charlotte to settle down into their new life. He had often been too generous for his own good – and hers.

"It's a shame that you still have to live with them," said Arial. "I think you deserve better."

Cinderella felt comforted by Arial's response. It made her feel less alone, and that meant a lot to her. When it came to how her stepfamily treated her, she had often wondered whether anyone – apart from Max, Phillip and Claire – would believe her.

"I wouldn't complain at staying here in this garden with you forever," said Cinderella.

"It's nice to be here with you," said Arial. "It's just us, and we're away from everything else on this beautiful night."

Cinderella would never have believed it if someone had told her that the ball was going to turn out to be so enlightening. The best she had been hoping for was simply to get away from the château for a while. She had never expected to actually click with anyone, and least of all, a princess.

"I hope it doesn't scare you by me saying so," announced Arial. "But meeting you tonight has been a big deal for me."

Arial couldn't help but take Cinderella's hands in hers. It wasn't long before the two women were holding each other tightly, their lips in contact and their eyes closed in a tranquil bliss.

Cruelly, the moment was taken away from them just as quickly as fate had granted it. As she heard the clock strike midnight, Cinderella froze in horror, realising that she had lost track of the time.

This was not good. This was not good at all.

Chapter Five

Cinderella quickly pulled herself away from Arial. She didn't want to, but she had to. Panic charged through every fibre of her being as she realised how easily she had lost track of the time. She was already supposed to be back. The kind old woman who had helped her get to the ball in the first place would be waiting for her.

Cinderella desperately didn't want to upset Arial, but she also didn't want to disrespect the very person who had made the night possible in the first place.

"Are you ok?" Arial asked, worried that Cinderella was having regrets about the kiss.

In a frenzy of exasperation, Cinderella couldn't even begin to explain herself.

"I'm really sorry," she stammered desperately as she backed frantically away from Arial. "I have to go."

She didn't want to abandon Arial but in a moment of panic, she felt as if she had no choice. She needed to get back to the old woman who had been so kind to her and there was no time to explain it all.

"Please don't go," Arial begged, scared that she had been too forward.

She tried to reach out towards Cinderella but the best she managed was to barely gloss over the maiden's gloved arm. Cinderella moved away at such a speed that it caused Arial to stumble forwards. All she could do was watch as Cinderella made a dash for it across the garden and into the palace.

Cinderella ran as fast as she could. She was keen to get away from Arial now – she didn't want to hurt or confuse her any more than she feared she had already. Struggling to run in the delicate finery of her ball gown and slippers, Cinderella thundered clumsily down the hallway. Suddenly, she could see the Duke approaching.

"Please slow down," he called. "Are you ok?"

Cinderella shot right past him and mumbled something incoherent about needing to get home. Tears were beginning to sting her eyes and her heart was beating fast, so much so that she would have struggled to talk coherently even if she wasn't running.

The Duke wasn't used to seeing anyone run through the hallways, and least of all a maiden who lived beyond the palace walls. Sensing that something wasn't right, he called out.

"Guards! Stop her!"

Knowing that the guards would be hot on her heels in no time at all, Cinderella ran faster than she ever thought was possible. She felt a small flash of relief once she got to the stairs that would lead her down and out of the palace, but she knew it was only a matter of time before someone would catch up to her if she didn't get a move on.

She ran and ran. Faster and faster. Losing her balance and almost falling over, she cursed herself for nearly hitting the floor completely. She was aware in that moment that she was without one of her slippers. She desperately wanted to go back and collect it in order that she could return it to the kind old lady. She knew the risk was too high though. To turn around to get the slipper was to risk getting caught. She was all the more worried by this point from having given the guards a reason to chase her.

Moments later, she could hear the Duke calling after her to tell her that she had left the slipper behind. Although he thought he was being helpful, it only served to heighten her fear, and made her run even more frantically.

In a twist of good fortune for Cinderella, the fact that she was now so late was such that the coachmen who had transported her to the ball were already waiting outside the palace for her. Seizing her opportunity and apologising profusely for her lateness, she swiftly hopped into the coach and moments later, the horses started to canter.

As the coach veered onwards and the palace was left further behind, Cinderella put her head in her hands.

"A good night then?" said one of the coachmen.

"It was wonderful. Thank you," blurted Cinderella. "I'm so sorry I'm so late. I didn't mean to keep you all."

"It's not ideal," the man said honestly. "But I'm sure now that you're here, we can get a speed on and get us all home soon enough."

"Thank you," said Cinderella.

For the rest of the journey, everyone sat in silence. The elegant rhythm of the horses' shoes against the road ahead could be heard above all else. The night was so clear that the sound had a timbre that was almost musical.

Cinderella's mind wandered. She wished with all her heart that her life could be less complicated. *Why does it feel like I've got hardly any control over my own destiny?* she thought. Lady Sharp had always been a bully and the way that her and her daughters had drained the family funds was such that Cinderella had not a penny to her name. She had nowhere else to go and no means of broadening her options. She had to live in the château with them. As much as it may have delighted her stepsisters to think of Cinderella living on the streets, they probably needed her to live with them in order that they could get her to do all of the housework.

Cinderella ached for a place of her own that she could truly call home. It didn't need to be a palace or even a château. Just a small cottage away from her horrible stepfamily would do nicely. Her mind wandered off further into thoughts of how amazing it would be to have Arial living there with her. That way, Arial would be free of the pressures of having to live up to the expectations of being a royal. The two of them could live peacefully together and not have to worry about what other people were going to demand of them next.

As the journey home came to an end, Cinderella thanked the men for their help. She quickly jumped out of the coach – and behind a bush – to get changed into an old, oversized dress that they had brought along for her. She folded the ball gown as neatly as she could in the circumstances and apologetically returned the one slipper that she hadn't lost in the palace.

"I'm so sorry about that," she said to the coachman.

He smiled reassuringly.

"Between you and me," he said. "I happen to know that Madam has lots of pairs of slippers and hardly gets to wear any of them nowadays. I'm sure she'll be ok with one less pair, and I know that she wanted you to have a good time. It looks like you did. Please don't be worried. We'll get home as quickly and as quietly as we can. It will all be ok."

Cinderella was grateful for his kind words. She thanked him quickly and made a dash for home. She wanted to sneak in unnoticed without the stress of having to face her stepfamily. She didn't want their horrible attitude to sour what had been –

overall – a wonderful night.

No such luck though.

As she slowly crept into the château, she was greeted by the mocking glares of Lady Sharp, Holly and Charlotte.

"Had a good night, did we?" Lady Sharp asked condescendingly.

Cinderella was too startled to respond. She always tried to avoid confrontation and although she was working incredibly hard not to show it, she was disgusted with Lady Sharp for being so rude. The words that Cinderella really wanted to say to her weren't a patch on what she actually managed to say.

"Yes, thank you," she said.

It took every ounce of her determination to keep things civil. She didn't want to offer any details. It made no sense to her to tell her stepfamily anything that they could use against her, or mock her for.

The fact that it was so late in the night went in Cinderella's favour. No more was said and with a nonchalant wave of Lady Sharp's hand, she was dismissed.

She walked upstairs promptly without wishing to draw further attention. As soon as she closed the door of her bedroom behind her, she sighed heavily – partly with relief and partly with emotion. How she wished that she hadn't had to leave Arial alone in the garden – especially because she hadn't managed to explain to her what was really going on. It scared Cinderella to think that perhaps Arial thought less of her for it.

She thought back to how enticing it had felt to be in Arial's company. She promised herself that even though everything felt so confusing and uncertain, she would try to get some sleep. She hoped that she would dream about Arial; her warm smile, her comforting scent and her soft lips. And her eyes – those gorgeous soulful eyes that spoke so many words and emotions. Cinderella had always felt that she was pretty good at reading other people, but when she had been talking with Arial, it was as if she could read her on a deeper level. She was used to having a just-about-acceptable rapport with her stepfamily and a good one with her friends but with Arial, it had felt so different – almost like seeing things through a whole spectrum of colours that she had never known to exist before.

As she scrambled into her makeshift bed and pulled the scratchy rags over her, Cinderella was looking forward to getting some rest. Her mind was impossibly busy though. She almost couldn't bear the thought of how upon waking at sunrise, everything would be back to normal; the normal that she had to endure under the dominance of her stepfamily.

****

Morning came soon enough, and as she had feared, the new day after the ball felt just like any other. As always, Cinderella knew that her time would be dedicated to the demands of Lady Sharp, Holly and Charlotte. There was nothing she could do about it. No matter how magical the ball had been, no matter how intensively she had felt a connection with Arial, there was nothing that Cinderella could do to hold on to those feelings of happiness and comfort. It was all over. Dragging herself through the tedium of her chores, she told herself that her only option was to move on.

As the day continued, Cinderella couldn't stop thinking about Arial and how amazing it had been to meet her. *What is she doing now? Is she thinking about me?* she wondered. The Princess had been in her dreams. Just thinking about the touch of her hand brought a feeling of warmth that Cinderella had never experienced before.

Throughout the course of the day, Cinderella went

from feeling that it was hopeless, to deciding that no matter what, she needed to see Arial again. It didn't even need to be immediately – nothing as rash and as frantic as that. It was too much of a big deal to risk getting it wrong. *Surely the universe will come through for me, just this once?* Cinderella mused. She had to believe in the possibility. She had to... She had to...

Chapter Six

The following day, Cinderella had an abundance of work to do. Elaborate breakfast requests – combined with the huge pile of clothes to be ironed – were such that she didn't have the luxury of time. In the flurry of attending to all of the women in the household except herself, her mind was far too occupied to be able to spare a thought for anything that she truly cared about. She had to run around the château to tidy up after everyone else. Clothes were scattered across different rooms and strewn messily over furniture, whilst dirty plates had been lazily placed anywhere at random. If it wasn't for her, the château would look tremendously unkempt. Her stepsisters had no respect for it. It made her sad to think what her father would say if he could see it.

Cinderella knew full well that some of the clothes that had been put out for her to wash had barely been worn, if at all. Her stepfamily had always been in the habit of giving her more work to do just for the fun of it. As much as Cinderella sometimes wanted to, she knew that calling any of her stepfamily out on their sly little games would only result in more trouble overall. In that regard, as much as she loathed it, it made sense to Cinderella to simply keep her head down and avoid making a fuss.

Upon hearing a knock at the front door, she was grateful for the distraction. She was already moving to answer it when she heard her stepmother squawking at her to do so.

"Just a moment," Cinderella called, not only to the person behind the door, but also in the hope of reassuring Lady Sharp.

When she opened the door, Cinderella was pleased to see Max, Phillip and Claire. The three of them were stood there eagerly, waiting to hear the details of what the ball had been like. They wanted to know if everything had gone ok for their friend, and whether her stepfamily had behaved.

"Well?" Claire asked expectantly. "How was it?"

"Tell us," said Max. "We're bursting to know. We're all ears."

Phillip playfully waggled his ears at Max's comment. He always knew how to make

Cinderella laugh.

Craning her head back to check that her stepfamily were preoccupied with whatever it was that they were doing, once she felt comfortable that the coast was clear, Cinderella motioned to her friends to step back from the door. She didn't want to run the risk of her stepfamily being able to overhear any of the conversation.

"I hate to tell you this," Cinderella said sincerely. "But the work that you all did on my dress went to ruin."

"How come?" Claire asked, concerned.

"It's horrible to have to say it," said Cinderella. "But Charlotte and Holly ripped it to shreds."

"No way?!" Max exclaimed, shocked. "What nasty pieces of work they are!"

"So you didn't get to go to the ball?" Claire asked.

Her friends looked so sad and worried. Cinderella didn't want them to feel that way, and so she quickly embraced the opportunity to tell them about the kind old woman who had stepped in to help at the last minute. She told them about how lucky she had been to get to the ball. Not only that, but she told them all about how amazing it had been to meet Arial, and how sad it had made her when she'd had to dash off so quickly into the night.

Claire had always been incredibly perceptive, and on this occasion, there was no exception.

"It sounds like you really like her," she said to Cinderella.

Cinderella already felt that the word "like" was certainly something of an understatement. As a result, she found herself shifting her weight from one foot to the other. As she shyly bowed her head, her long hair failed to cover the blush in her cheeks. She wanted to be with Arial. So much. The feeling was overwhelming and undeniable. There was something about being in her company that had been emotionally fulfilling beyond words. Cinderella wished so badly that she could be holding Arial again and kissing her softly. She had grown confident that Arial felt the same. It was, after all, Arial who had first leaned in towards her for a kiss.

Cinderella's three friends watched her with intrigue. They had never seen her like this before. She seemed distracted, as if her soul was on a different plane to the harsh realities of having to serve her horrible stepfamily.

"Anyway," said Max. "We've got a letter for you."

He reached into his bag, keen to avoid being late for all the other stops the trio had yet to cover on their delivery round.

"Me?" asked Cinderella.

"Well, not you personally," he said, laughing playfully. "Unless you happened to lose a slipper at the palace when you went to the ball?"

"What?! You're kidding?!" said Cinderella, genuinely shocked.

She grabbed the letter out of her friend's hand and opened it straight away. Her eyes darted across the neatly-handwritten message:

Are you missing a slipper? If so, we are looking for you. Princess Arial wishes to find the maiden who lost one at the ball. Every maiden in the kingdom will be given the opportunity to present the slipper that matches with the one that was found at the palace.

Cinderella couldn't believe her eyes.

"But this must mean..." she stammered. "This must mean that Arial is looking for me!"

"Yes, it sounds like she is," Claire said.

"But that must mean..."

"She likes you," Claire interrupted, pleased that she could confirm the exciting news to Cinderella.

"I can't believe it," said Cinderella. "I wouldn't have blamed her for being mad at me for how I ran off. I knew she liked me, but I would have never expected her to actively come looking for me, not in a million years."

"Stranger things have happened," Claire said, laughing a little.

"Wait! There's more!" said Cinderella.

She fumbled frantically with the piece of paper in her hands to read what was on the other side of it.

"Go on," said Max.

Cinderella read on, her eyes widening in shock and excitement.

If it's your slipper, the palace hereby declares that

Princess Arial asks for your hand in marriage.

"Marriage?!" exclaimed Cinderella. "That's beyond my wildest dreams!"

She stopped to think about it for a moment. How could someone like Arial want to marry her? A princess marrying a maiden: it was simply unheard of. Besides, Lady Sharp would never allow it.

And then, in a moment of inspiration, something powerful dawned on Cinderella: should she agree to get married to Arial, she could walk the palace grounds with her beloved every day. They would look after each other – emotionally and practically. It would be beautiful.

"This is all so much to take in," said Cinderella, her head whirling with a million thoughts amongst the intensity of yearning for Arial. "And anyway, I'll never be allowed to leave the château in order to present myself to the palace."

"You don't have to worry about that," said Max, acknowledging Cinderella's predicament. "Representatives of the palace will be doing the rounds tomorrow. They're planning to stop by at every house in the kingdom."

"Tomorrow feels like ages away," Cinderella said

excitedly. "I wish I didn't have to keep Arial waiting. I wish I could go to the palace today."

Claire raised an eyebrow at Cinderella. It was the perfect cue to persuade her to slow down and think for a moment. It would be difficult to sneak out of the château unnoticed, even if the risk did feel worth it.

Cinderella figured that in order to avoid making her stepfamily suspicious of her pending escape, she would need, for the time being, to carry on as normal – with compliance and dignity. If she could pull this off, she knew that she'd never have to do the same amount of housework in her life ever again. Not only that, but she would never have to so much as set eyes on her horrible stepfamily again.

Shaking her head, Cinderella was still far too excited to be able to tell whether or not she was thinking straight about the whole thing.

"What do you think?" she addressed her friends. "Do you think once the three witches have settled down for the evening, I should make a break for it and head to the palace?"

"Too right!" Phillip said, loud and enthusiastic.

Cinderella was grateful to her friends. They were always so supportive. She clapped her hands together gleefully. Claire looked at her pointedly. They both knew that she would have to conceal her excitement from her stepfamily in order for her plan to work.

The thought of being able to see Arial again made Cinderella so happy. On top of that, the thought of actually being able to marry her so that they could be together forever made for an incredible feeling. She needed things to go right when it came to escaping her stepfamily. There was so much to lose.

Cinderella hugged her friends tightly.

"Don't panic if you can't get in touch with me for a while," she said. "You know I'll let you all know I'm ok, just as soon as I possibly can."

Her friends hugged her back with an extra squeeze. They were on Cinderella's side entirely and knew what was at stake. They wanted so much for her to be happy. They wanted her to be able to live joyfully without her stepfamily's bitterness and hatred dragging her down.

Waving goodbye to her friends until they were out of sight, Cinderella took the opportunity to compose herself before walking back up the pathway and through the front door. Once inside, she went upstairs to give Lady Sharp the message.

"It's from the palace," said Cinderella, in the most neutral tone she could muster.

Lady Sharp peered down at the piece of paper. She didn't even bother to look at Cinderella.

"I see," she said, seeming uninterested. "You have to give Tiffany a bath today. She smells dreadful."

Cinderella was certain that the poor cat knew she was being talked about unfavourably.

"Ok," said Cinderella.

Compliantly, she quickly left the room to get started on the housework. She told herself that if she took things one room at a time, it would help her to keep her mind focused on the bigger picture. She washed the clothes in hot soapy water and hung them out to dry. She ironed them carefully – even the ones that didn't need ironing, as per her stepfamily's instructions – and then neatly folded them. There was even a part of her that wanted to do the best job she had ever done, purely for old times' sake and as something of a leaving present to her stepfamily; there was no way that she would want to see them again, not after all they had done to her with their horrible attitude and comments.

As much as she wanted to stay focused on planning her escape, Cinderella found her mind wandering off to somewhere else. She enjoyed re-living her dance with Arial. Scenes of the smiling Princess floated through her head as she swept the landing. She was in such a beautiful place in her fantasies that when Lady Sharp stormed out of her room – slamming the door behind her – it startled the younger woman all the more.

Cinderella braced herself, expecting to be shouted at for something that was probably not her fault.

Lady Sharp stood quietly with a thunderous expression across her face. She glared at Cinderella disapprovingly. Suddenly, a smile started to flicker out from the corners of her thin-lipped mouth.

"I want you to go up into the loft for me," she said cunningly. "Going through all of my dresses for the ball the other day made me wonder about the ones I haven't worn for a while. I want you to bring them all down so I can try them on."

Cinderella felt anxious. She feared that it was going to be a long afternoon.

I guess the sweeping will have to wait, she thought. *Oh well, if that's what the sour-faced one wants…* Cinderella willed herself not to giggle. She didn't usually allow herself to think in such terms, but she figured that it didn't matter so much now that she would be leaving her stepfamily behind soon enough.

The wooden ladder up to the loft was so rickety that Cinderella silently prayed that it would hold her weight. She wasn't a big woman by any means, but the creaking sound that came from each rung made her very aware that it wouldn't take much for the aged material to snap.

Lady Sharp stood patiently at the base of the ladder. Her arms were folded as if to state that she was far too important and superior to even think about helping Cinderella. Cinderella was too busy trying to distribute her weight evenly during her climb that she didn't notice, not that it would have surprised her of course.

Cinderella scrambled into the loft's small entrance hatch, relieved to be finished with the ladder. She turned around to let Lady Sharp know that she would do her best to find all of the dresses for her.

No such luck though. Instead of being willing to entertain any conversation of such nature, Lady

Sharp nonchalantly pulled the ladder away.

Cinderella had no hope of being able to get down without it. The best option available to her would now be to jump. However, the distance between the loft hatch and the floor was such that at minimum, the least of her worries would be one broken bone.

"What are you doing?" Cinderella asked, terrified and hoping that her suspicions were wrong.

Lady Sharp laughed sadistically, a gleeful glint in her eyes.

"You won't need this now," she said coldly. "You can stay up there for a while."

And with that, with the ladder in her hands, she started to walk away.

"Please let me out," Cinderella called down.

It was too late. Lady Sharp had already left the room. The only company Cinderella had was from the warmth of her tears as they ran freely down her cheeks.

Chapter Seven

Night had fallen some time ago and no longer was any daylight shining through the crack in the roof. Despite the absence of light though, Cinderella couldn't sleep. Her mind was taunted by the fact that, by now, she should have left the château and should have been reunited with Arial. To make matters worse, Cinderella hadn't heard anything from her stepfamily since finding herself trapped in the loft. She just knew that they would be plotting something awful for her; anything to sabotage her happiness, anything to keep her where they wanted her. They had always been bullies in every sense of the word.

With every hour of night that passed, Cinderella didn't sleep at all, and soon enough, there was once again a small glint of light coming in through the hole in the roof. She hoped that Arial was still waiting for her, but it scared her to think that if her stepfamily could have their way, she might not ever be able to see Arial again. *How cruel of them to intervene so callously*, Cinderella thought as she aggressively threw a stray piece of wood across the cavernous loft.

It wasn't often that Cinderella allowed herself to feel angry. She had become so used to suppressing such feelings over the years. She had learned a long time ago that getting angry wouldn't free her and would just eat away at her soul even more. She had always tried so hard to stay in touch with some kind of hope, willing herself to be patient. This time though, Lady Sharp had gone too far. *How dare she try and take away my one chance of happiness?!* Cinderella thought as she scowled at the dirt and grime that tainted her fingers.

Cinderella knew that the way she was feeling went beyond her desire to escape. This was about Arial. This was about the fact that there was an amazing woman out there – strong, kind and thoughtful – just waiting to be with her. Cinderella made a promise to herself that she couldn't let Arial down.

She was certain that her rapport – well, lack thereof – with her stepfamily was such that any hope of coming to an agreement with them would be in vain. In that regard, Cinderella told herself that although she would prefer not to, she would probably be willing to play dirty if she absolutely had to. She reasoned with herself that cutting ties with her stepfamily would be like ripping off a plaster: unpleasant in the moment but quick enough that once over, the relief would be tremendous.

With no other option, she started to think tactically. She figured that the roof couldn't be so sturdy as to be soundproof. She wasn't sure when Max, Claire and Phillip would next be nearby. After all, they were probably not expecting to hear from her for a few days.

Hmm… how could I get the attention of someone who might be able to help me? Cinderella considered.

Her mind started to whirl. It veered off on a number of tangents, each with an array of possibilities; there had to be a way to get out of the loft. Besides, surely her stepfamily would miss her soon enough, and would come to get her out when they needed her to cook them a decent meal. They were far too lazy to put the effort in themselves, and even if they wanted to go out for a meal, they would probably insist on Cinderella being around to help them get ready.

It scared Cinderella to think that maybe this was all a dream, and that maybe she hadn't really met someone as wonderful as Arial. After all, it wasn't unusual for her to have lovely thoughts, designed to take her away from reality for a while. But no, Arial must be real – Cinderella knew that her imagination was good, but it wasn't *that* good.

It inspired her to think about how amazing it would be to be married to Arial. Her mind began to wander off to somewhere comforting as she pictured what it could be like to wake up next to her. Seeing her glorious long locks cascading over a plump pillow, Cinderella would hold her tightly and then they would go downstairs to cook breakfast together.

She keenly indulged in her daydream. She tried to imagine how Arial might prefer her eggs to be cooked, and whether she preferred fruit juice or a cup of tea in the mornings, or perhaps a glass of milk. For Cinderella, every thought about Arial made the mundane seem interesting. She couldn't lie to herself; her feelings for Arial were substantial and like nothing she had ever felt before.

Reality snapped through the images in her mind – and redirected her focus – when she heard a loud knocking on the front door of the château. Whoever it was, sounded urgent in wanting to make their presence known. It frustrated Cinderella to think that all the way up in the loft, there was nothing she could do to get their attention. She had nothing with which to make a noise, and if she shouted at the top of her voice, it stood to reason that Holly would start singing (awfully, as she often did!) to drown the sound out.

It was clear to Cinderella that Lady Sharp had worked out what was going on and didn't want to lose control. Cinderella knew that although her stepmother was a lazy woman, she was a clever one too, and where she could manipulate a situation to her twisted idea of an advantage, she would.

All Cinderella could do was work especially hard to listen out for what was going on downstairs. She knew that the best she could hope for would be to merely hear whatever it was that she was missing out on.

****

Outside of the château, Max, Phillip and Claire were concerned that Cinderella hadn't answered the door. They knew that she hadn't been to the palace, because when out doing their rounds of the kingdom, they had seen that the search party for Arial's love interest was still ongoing. Having a strong knowledge of how Lady Sharp often liked to keep Cinderella locked in the château, it made sense to them to go back to check on her.

"She hasn't opened the door, but where else could she be?" Phillip asked.

"This is worrying," said Max. "This isn't like her at all."

"Let's check the garden," Claire said decisively.

In the large garden, the three of them shouted rigorously for Cinderella.

****

As he stood in the living room while Lady Sharp and her two daughters insisted that they knew nothing about the maiden in question, the Duke was becoming all the more irritated. He could tell that something wasn't right. He sensed that they were all trying too hard.

Sighing and not expecting to get anything useful from the three blabbering women, the Duke turned to leave when suddenly, there was a thunderous knock at the front door, one so demanding, that he instinctively went to respond to it himself.

Before Lady Sharp could do anything about it, Max, Phillip and Claire bounded into the hallway.

"Please, good Sir," Claire implored. "You have to

listen to us. The woman you are looking for is in this château. She often gets locked up. She must be in here somewhere."

"Are you sure?" the Duke asked sceptically. "The situation sounds incredibly unusual. How could she have got to the ball if what you are saying is true?"

Claire sighed, exasperated.

"The slipper!" prompted Max. "Tell him about the slipper!"

"Yes! The slipper!" Claire exclaimed, suddenly getting her thoughts together. "You remember, don't you Sir, running in the palace, after the woman you are looking for, demanding that she turn around and come back for her slipper? Well, truthfully, I'm not sure that she has the other half of the pair anymore. It's a long story, but trust me, if you see her, there's a fair chance that you'll recognise her. Princess Arial certainly would."

"And where is this elusive slipper-less woman of whom you speak?" the Duke asked doubtfully.

Claire didn't need to say anything else. In that very moment, Cinderella's calls for help could be heard against the silence of the stunned household.

Chapter Eight

It concerned the Duke tremendously to think that a woman had been shut away in a loft – in her own home of all places! Much to his dismay though, that's how he found Cinderella. Lady Sharp, as much as she liked to be in control and was usually good at manipulating a situation in her favour, was embarrassed into fetching the ladder that she had hidden away. Max, Claire and Phillip told the Duke everything, and in their refusal to leave the château until the loft had been checked, Cinderella's stepmother was outnumbered.

As the Duke carried the ladder to the loft himself, Cinderella's three friends bounded along with him, elaborating on the young woman's unfortunate situation. Lady Sharp and her two daughters could do nothing but reluctantly follow the search party. Unsure of what to do in the highly unusual situation, between them, they hoped that Cinderella wouldn't mind covering for them; she had done so before.

Cinderella could have cried with relief when she realised that she was going to be rescued. *To think that I was almost too scared to shout for help!* she thought. Had she remained silent, it wouldn't have been through any desire to defend her wicked stepfamily's awful behaviour.

Once Cinderella had climbed down the ladder, Claire welcomed her with a hug.

"I'm so glad you're ok," Claire said. "I was so worried about you."

Max and Phillip nodded in agreement.

"Is it true?" the Duke asked.

"Is what true?" asked Cinderella.

"Well," the Duke replied bluntly. "Your friends here tell me that your family aren't very nice to you."

Before Cinderella could collect her thoughts to offer a response, Holly promptly interjected.

"Lies! All lies! Mother, tell them!"

Lady Sharp shot a forceful look in Cinderella's direction.

"Excuse me!" said the Duke, trying to take control of the situation. "Cinderella hasn't said anything yet. For goodness' sake, please allow her to speak."

All eyes were on Cinderella. She knew that having come this far, it was the best chance that she was ever going to have of being able to get away from her stepfamily. Equally though, she was still reluctant to say anything that would humiliate them in front of the Duke. As she looked at the scowl that spread across Charlotte's face, it reminded her of how hateful her stepfamily had always been towards her, and of how she had often wondered whether they had any love in their hearts at all.

Cinderella's stunned silence was such that the Duke decided to try a different approach.

"Tell me about the slipper," he said.

"Ok," said Cinderella. "It's a long story, but do you remember when I passed you in the palace hallway as I tried to get away from the ball?"

The Duke nodded, listening attentively.

"And do you remember how I stumbled before losing the slipper? It was somewhere along the hallway where the red carpet ends and the tiling towards the steps down and out of the palace begins."

"Yes," the Duke said excitedly, a joyful smile on his face.

"Well," said Cinderella, proud and relieved. "You must know that it was I who lost the slipper. Who else would be able to tell you *exactly* where in the palace they were when they stumbled whilst running away? I can even tell you what the guards looked like. One had a beard and the other looked – and I don't wish to offend anyone by saying this – a little overweight."

The Duke laughed, impressed with Cinderella's candour. Suddenly though, he was hit with a feeling of uncertainty.

"How do I know that you're not telling me this based on something that you may have heard from somebody else?" he asked.

It was a good question. Holly took the opportunity to butt in.

"You see, it couldn't have been her slipper. She's lying. What princess would want to be with her anyway? She's not even that pretty."

Lady Sharp smiled, pleased at her daughter's

attempt to undermine Cinderella's account of events.

Of course! Cinderella thought, *Arial!*

"I promise that I'm usually very good at keeping a secret," said Cinderella. "But just this once, if it helps to clear things up, I'll tell you about Arial. Her favourite meal is spaghetti bolognaise, and her favourite flowers are sunflowers. I know this because she told me that she always has her favourite meal on a Wednesday, and that through her bedroom window, is a glorious view of the sunflowers outside. How would I know such details had I not been talking to her all night at the ball?"

"It sounds like you know her better than I do," said the Duke.

He wanted to believe Cinderella, he really did. He still wasn't quite sure though, much to Cinderella's anxiety and to Lady Sharp's satisfaction.

Calmly, Cinderella put her hands on the Duke's shoulders, keen to address him personally and casting aside the fact that he was from the palace.

"Listen to me," she said. "I love her. I love Arial."

The Duke didn't want to bring the wrong maiden to meet the Princess, especially seeing that the stakes were so high. Despite this, he was beginning to deeply believe that Cinderella was telling the truth.

"Come with me," he said. "The Princess is waiting."

"Really?!" Cinderella exclaimed, clasping her hands joyfully together and almost bouncing up and down with excitement.

"Yes," the Duke replied. "She told us that upon finding the maiden in question, we are to escort her to the palace at once. I am now convinced that the maiden in question is you. We should be on our way. The Princess has been so distracted lately and we don't want to keep her waiting a moment longer."

As Cinderella began to follow the Duke's lead, Lady Sharp spoke up.

"I don't think so," she said, her tone acidic and cold.

She wasn't going to let Cinderella leave so easily. She moved to stand in between her stepdaughter and the Duke. Before she could though, Cinderella stepped to the side, suddenly experiencing a feeling of empowerment; she knew that she would be leaving her stepfamily behind, and she was looking forward to a beautiful future. Her feelings for Arial had given her that final push that she vitally needed to be able to stand up to her stepfamily.

"It's over," said Cinderella. "I'm leaving. You've always gone out of your way to be unpleasant towards me, as have Holly and Charlotte. I've only ever tried to be nice to you, and still you've taken great efforts over the years to treat me horribly. When Father married you, I was so excited to think that I was going to have a stepmother and two stepsisters, but over the years you have all... Ugh!"

Cinderella paused for a moment, struggling to gather her thoughts.

"You know," she said. "I've got nothing else to say. You can't control me anymore. I'm going now."

An overwhelming feeling of relief flooded through every fibre of Cinderella's being. Years of pain and frustration seemed to visibly lift from her shoulders. She felt lighter somehow. In contrast, Lady Sharp's expression turned from one of coldness to one of absolute shock. For the first time in a very long time, Cinderella found herself able to hold eye contact with her stepmother. She wasn't afraid of her anymore. For perhaps the first time in her life, Cinderella felt sorry for her stepmother. *How awful it must be to hold so much misplaced hatred*, she thought.

"And to think that I could have thrown you out on the streets when your father died," said Lady Sharp. "You've always been spoilt and ungrateful."

Cinderella chewed on her lower lip for a moment, infuriated, but unsure as to whether she should even bother to dignify Lady Sharp's awful comment with a response.

"That's rich coming from a woman who deems it appropriate to imprison me in the loft," she finally said.

"She's got you there," Max piped up.

The Duke nodded in agreement.

"You can't leave, and that's final," Lady Sharp insisted. "Besides, you're deluded if you think that a princess would really be interested in you."

There was nothing else to say. Cinderella trusted Arial so much more than she could ever trust her stepfamily. Arial's kindness had told Cinderella all that she needed to know.

"Cinderella," said the Duke. "The Princess hasn't stopped talking about you since the ball. She has been beside herself with worry about not being able to find you."

"I feel the same way about her," said Cinderella.

As she turned to face her stepsisters, she felt sorry for them too, perhaps even more so than she did for Lady Sharp.

"You both know that you haven't been good to me," said Cinderella. "I won't insult everyone here by inviting you to debate me on that. Look, you should get yourselves some friends. Be kind to each other and don't be like your mother. For goodness' sake, give yourselves some dignity."

The two sisters looked at each other, stunned and confused. Whether or not they had the propensity to change for the better, Cinderella was glad to have given them something to think about.

Cinderella sighed. Her emotions were running high and she was beginning to feel drained. She knew though, that she was doing the right thing. She could feel it in her heart and in her soul. She turned to address Max, Claire and Phillip.

"I love you all," she said. "Thank you, for

everything. I'll see you all soon."

With that, the Duke led Cinderella out of the château, down the path and towards the carriage that was waiting for her. The horses at the front of it looked majestic, their glossy coats sparkling in the sun.

Once they were in the carriage and on their way, Cinderella put her head in her hands. She didn't want to be rude to the Duke though. She felt that she owed him an explanation, especially considering the scene he had just witnessed. She needn't have worried though. He was keen to assure her that no matter what she had experienced before, her life with Arial was going to be wonderful. Cinderella believed him completely. She had been thinking about exactly the same thing for days.

"Thank you for helping me," she said to the Duke. "Your patience made all the difference."

"You're welcome," he replied. "There's a lot to look forward to."

As the horses cantered elegantly onwards, Cinderella was beginning to feel a sense of hope. Although she was still shaken from the confrontation that she had just endured, she felt proud for having finally stood up to her stepfamily. Taking a deep breath, she willed herself not to dwell on the past – she didn't want it to cause her any more pain. She was ready to begin a new life – one that would be filled with love, kindness and understanding.

Chapter Nine

As soon as Cinderella stepped out of the carriage, she felt nervous. Although she hadn't stopped thinking about Arial for days, it suddenly felt as if she was about to meet the Princess for the first time. She didn't know quite what to expect; would it be different? Would they still connect with each other in the way that they had at the ball?

The enormity of the situation hit Cinderella like a ton of bricks; not only had she left everything that she had ever known behind, but she had burned that bridge well and truly. Her stepfamily wouldn't take her back. Well, maybe they would if she begged them, but they would be certain to make it difficult for her.

"Come with me," said the Duke.

He gestured for Cinderella to follow him. She found herself walking up the steps leading into the palace. As she ascended, her mind darted back to the memory of what it had been like to run down them when she had charged away from the ball. It felt different to be walking up the steps and towards something amazing, rather than running away with anxiety and fear. Cinderella smiled to herself. She knew that every step was taking her closer to her beloved. It felt like she was in a dream. So much had happened, within a matter of days. Instinctively though, she felt that she had made the right choice.

She paused for a moment.

"Are you ok?" the Duke asked.

"I am, I promise I am," she said. "It just feels so surreal. This is such a big thing. I haven't stopped thinking about what it might feel like to see the Princess again. And now that I'm finally going to, I just feel so emotional about all of it."

"Ok," said the Duke. "I'll tell you something. Listen. I'm convinced that the Princess is nervous about seeing you again too. Think about it. She's gone through so much to get you to the palace that if it were to go wrong, not only would it hurt her personally, but it would be something of a public humiliation for her, considering how many people in the kingdom have been made aware of her search for you."

"Wow," said Cinderella. "I had never thought of it like that before."

Although it was her second visit to the palace, Cinderella was still awestruck at how lavish the inside of it was. She still couldn't quite believe the fact that this could soon be her home. She wasn't too bothered about that side of things though. Her main need was to be with Arial. To be loved is all she had ever wanted. It felt almost strange to her that in just mere moments, she would be standing in front of the woman who had made her feel not only appreciated, but worthy.

The Duke led Cinderella up another flight of stairs. It spiralled around a marble pillar. Golden banisters led the way along the plush red carpet that covered the white floor tiles. Cinderella hadn't seen this part of the palace before. She figured that it must have been out of bounds to the guests at the ball.

"This is amazing," she said to the Duke. "I thought the palace was big when I was at the ball that night, but seeing it like this, it's more than I could have imagined."

"It won't be long until you're with the Princess," the Duke replied. "We've got just one more hallway ahead of us and then we'll be at her room."

The rest of the journey passed by in a blur. The anticipation gave Cinderella a spring in her step.

Once she found herself stood waiting outside Arial's room, the Duke knocked on the door.

Arial must have been waiting right behind the door, just bursting to open it to finally see her love again.

"It's you, it's you! You're really here!" Arial exclaimed excitedly.

She was so overcome with emotion, and trying hard not to cry. But more than that, the first thing she needed to do was to wrap her arms around Cinderella. She had so much to tell her, and so much to ask her.

The Duke looked relieved to see Arial happier than he had known her to be in a long time. He graciously bowed and then excused himself.

"I'll be on my way now," he said. "I must let your father know that Cinderella is here. He will be pleased."

Once the Duke had gone, Arial invited Cinderella into the room.

"I didn't even catch your name when I met you,"

Arial said. "I was so afraid that I'd never get to see you again."

"I'm so sorry to have worried you like that," said Cinderella. "You really made an impact on me. And I desperately didn't want to run off like that at the ball. I promise you I had my reasons though. I had to get back home. It's so complicated. I promise I'll tell you all about it, but please, do know that my need to dash off when the clock struck midnight wasn't due to any ill feeling towards you."

Arial smiled at Cinderella.

"I know. I trust you," she said. "It's hard for me to describe, but I've just got this intuitive feeling that I can trust you."

Cinderella beamed from ear to ear.

"I know exactly what you mean," she said. "It's like there's an energy between us. I can't quite put it into words either. But I've never felt anything like this before. It feels amazing."

Arial sat down on her bed and took Cinderella by the hands. She guided her to sit down next to her.

"Your room is beautiful," said Cinderella. "You can

tell that it's yours; you've got a mural of sunflowers on the wall."

"Yes," said Arial. "I painted that myself. I love painting, probably almost as much as I love gardening. I can't wait to share my passions with you."

"I feel exactly the same way," Cinderella said ecstatically. "There's so much more that I want to know about you. I've got so much to tell you."

Arial gave Cinderella's hand a squeeze. It felt just as comforting to the two of them as it had done that night when they had walked the palace garden.

"You do know that marriage is forever, don't you?" Arial enquired. "I really do want to spend the rest of my life with you. I can feel it."

"I couldn't stop thinking about you," said Cinderella.

She lovingly curled her fingers around a lock of Arial's hair and gazed with wonder into her eyes. It was such a relief to be back with her.

"It has been the same way for me," said Arial. "When you had to leave the ball so promptly, I was so scared that I'd never get to see you again. I didn't know why you had to run, but it looked urgent. I was worried about you."

It made Cinderella feel sad to think that she had caused so much worry to Arial. That was the last thing that she wanted to do. And so, taking a deep breath, she didn't want to spoil the moment by offloading everything, but she was certainly keen to explain at least some of what had happened that night.

"It was something outside of my control that I desperately needed to attend to," she said. "I promise to tell you everything. It might take some time, but I promise that I will. You were perfect – in every way – that night. I really didn't want to leave. But... oh my goodness I'm just so glad to be back with you."

As Cinderella looked around at the splendour of Arial's bedroom, something suddenly dawned on her.

"I have to tell you something," she said. "I don't have a lot of money. In fact, I have none. I think it's only fair to tell you that I'm not quite sure how I could contribute financially – certainly not compared to what you're used to anyway."

"Hey," said Arial, sensitive to what Cinderella was

saying. "That's not a problem at all. I just really, really want you as a person. I want you for who you are. That's all that matters to me. And that's why I haven't been able to stop thinking about you since we first met."

Arial's revelation made it easy for Cinderella to be candid.

"I love you," she whispered as she squeezed Arial's hand in hers.

It was the perfect opportunity for Arial to admit her feelings to Cinderella.

"To be honest," she said. "I sensed that I loved you as soon as I first laid eyes on you. It's difficult to describe, but, well... yes."

The two of them laughed. Not from embarrassment, but just from the sheer pleasure of knowing that they were both on the same page.

Arial cupped her warm hands around Cinderella's face. The two of them shuffled closer together until they were holding each other in a secure embrace.

"I'm so happy," Cinderella whispered, full of emotion.

"Me too," said Arial. "Seeing that we're going to get married, I want to introduce you to my family. Would you be ok with that? The palace is so big that there really is no rush to meet them, you know, if you don't quite feel ready for that yet."

"No, no, I'd love to meet them," said Cinderella. "I've already seen them at the ball and it makes sense to become acquainted. I know that we're both moving pretty fast but it's clear that our feelings are true, and so there's no time like the present. I can't wait to be with you forever."

****

Arial led Cinderella through several hallways and, eventually, into a large room. There were three thrones there. The King was sat on the one in the middle. The size of the room was such that every step Cinderella took echoed and bounced around the walls as she walked towards the King. Despite her nervous train of thought, she was soon made to feel welcome.

"Ah, so this is who you've been talking about, Arial," said the King, his tone warm and enthusiastic.

He jumped up to a standing position, clapping his hands together. He was an old man, but he didn't hold back when feeling inspired.

Instinctively, Cinderella curtsied.

"It's an honour to meet you, Your Highness. My name is Cinderella."

She extended her hand towards him, not quite sure of how to address a king, having never done so before. She needn't have worried though. He was enchanted by her humble mannerisms. Not only that, but it quickly became apparent to Cinderella that he was a very approachable person.

"It's brilliant to meet you," he said. "Arial is so taken with you. She hasn't stopped talking about you since the ball. I know I did the right thing in sending a search party out to find you. I haven't seen Arial this happy in a long time."

"I'm so sorry if I caused you to worry at all," Cinderella said to the King.

She was keen to make a good first impression, but equally, she really meant it.

"Oh no, not at all, don't worry about it," said the King. "The important thing is that you're here now. Arial tells me that she would like to take your hand in marriage. Is this something that you would like?"

"Oh yes," said Cinderella. "More than anything."

"There hasn't been a wedding in the family for quite some time," said the King. "I'm tremendously excited about this. Whatever my daughter wants, she will have. There's no time like the present to start preparing."

The King signalled to the Duke to fetch a quill and a scroll.

Turning towards Cinderella, Arial smiled.

"You do know that upon marrying me, your title will be that of Princess Cinderella, don't you? Are you ok with that?"

Cinderella paused, allowing the new and unusual thought to tumble around in her mind. She expected that a title would take her a while to become acquainted – and indeed, familiar – with.

"Well, it's certainly going to be very new to me," she told Arial honestly.

"Oh, that's fine," said Arial. "The important thing is that we're going to be together for a very long time. You'll have plenty of time to get used to your title, and I sense that, eventually, you'll embrace it. You deserve the very best. We're going to have a beautiful wedding ceremony, and a lovely party. I want you to invite your friends. I sense that you might not want to invite everyone you know though."

"I don't think I'll be inviting my stepfamily," said Cinderella. "But I'd like my good friends – Max, Claire and Phillip – to be there, and also, the kind woman who helped me get to the ball in the first place, as well as her coachmen and footman. That's really important to me. Without them, none of this would have been possible."

"Wonderful," said the King. "I will arrange all of that for you. The Duke will send the invites out promptly."

Cinderella and Arial excitedly wrapped their arms around each other and jumped with joy. The lengths that they'd had to go to in order to be together would soon be a footnote in their love story. It had taken a lot to get to this point, but it had all been worth it. They both had a lot to look forward to.

Chapter Ten

The days leading up to the wedding passed quickly. Cinderella was filled with happiness as she and Arial prepared for their special day. Everyone in the kingdom was invited, with the exception of Lady Sharp, Holly and Charlotte. Cinderella was determined that when it came to those who were going to be her personal guests, she only wanted people who fully supported the marriage to be in attendance.

On the morning of the wedding, there was still some fine-tuning to do. The palace staff ran around frantically to ensure that everything would go to plan. The Duke was marvellous, carefully following every detailed order that Arial had put to him.

Cinderella had been assigned an entire team to help her get ready. It was their job to help her get into her wedding gown, and to assist with her hair and makeup. Nothing was overlooked and no expense was spared.

As she caught sight of herself in the mirror, she was overcome with emotion. Although she had felt glamorous when she had got dressed for the ball, the haphazard challenges of getting there had been such that she had never truly had the time to take it all in. Looking in the mirror to observe how her wedding dress looked, a sense of calmness washed over her.

Her mind turned to the fact that her parents couldn't be with her for such a special day. Although she still missed them terribly, she knew they would have been proud of her. They had always wanted her to be happy.

The rest of the morning passed by in a surreal haze, so much so that Cinderella was barely able to take any of it in.

She was pleased to see that Max, Phillip, and Claire – as well as the old woman and her assistants – were in attendance. Cinderella had put in a good word for her three friends and as a result, they presented in new clothes. They all looked smart. Not only that, but everybody was beaming from ear to ear.

Once everyone was gathered in the church, the Vicar's voice was loud enough to command the room. Cinderella and Arial smiled at each other.

They were both so certain from deep within their souls that they were doing something magical together. The love between the two of them was out of this world. They both knew it was special. Cinderella knew that the love Arial showed her was so far beyond the limitations of what her stepfamily had. Equally, Arial felt strongly that Cinderella understood her in a way that nobody else ever had before. They both meant so much to each other. They looked slightly nervous, but no more so than any two people would, given that they were about to say their vows in front of an audience. Still though, they were in a loving, supportive environment, surrounded by people who genuinely wanted the best for them.

"Arial," said the Vicar. "Do you take Cinderella to be your wife?"

"I do," she replied, wiping a couple of tears away from her eyes.

She was blissfully happy. The King had already promised her that he would stop demanding that she live up to her reputation as a princess. He wanted her to have time and space to be with Cinderella.

"Cinderella," the Vicar said as he turned to face her. "Do you take Arial to be your wife?"

Cinderella was as tearful as Arial. She had never felt so sure of anything before in her life.

"I do," she said with conviction.

"I now pronounce you married to each other," the Vicar declared.

Cinderella and Arial jumped to hold each other in a tight embrace. Arial cupped her hands around Cinderella's face. She then leaned in towards her and the two of them shared the most passionate kiss before charging away down the aisle.

The crowd cheered.

"Such a happy couple," said the old lady as she smiled at Cinderella's three friends.

They all agreed.

It wasn't long after that everybody gathered for the wedding reception, which took place in the very same room as the ball had. The food was delicious. The music played by the orchestra was grand. The Prince was there too. Unlike when he had been at the ball, he looked relieved that, on this occasion, he didn't have to impress anybody. Perhaps the King had decided to go easier on all of his children, knowing that when the time was right for them, they would find the love that they needed.

The King walked around the room, keen to be a good host and to ensure that everybody was having a good time. In that regard, considering his position, he was very approachable to the people of the kingdom.

"You've made Arial so happy," he told Cinderella. "Welcome to the family."

Cinderella smiled. It felt wonderful to be accepted. She confidently tapped a spoon against her champagne glass, emoted to address the room.

"Thank you all so much for being here to celebrate our special day with us. I wouldn't be here at all if it wasn't for all of you. You all played an essential part in making today possible. You all helped me to get to the ball, which enabled me to meet Arial. You all helped me to get away from my horrible stepfamily at a time when it really mattered – more than it ever had before. I promise that now I'm a princess, I will do everything I possibly can to help you all. Please know that if there's anything you ever need – no matter how big or how small it may feel – *please* do ask me, because I will forever be in your debts, all of you."

As the celebrations continued, everybody sang and

danced joyfully. They were happy for Cinderella and Arial, and they were having a lovely time.

"It's a bit warm in here," Arial said to Cinderella after they had finished a dance. "Shall we go outside for a bit?"

"I'd like that," Cinderella replied.

Smiling softly, she was ready to take a small break from the hustle and bustle of the room. She was enjoying every moment, but the thought of sharing a nice quiet one with her new wife was impossible to resist.

As she had done at the ball, Arial took Cinderella by the hand and led her gracefully out into the palace garden. Red and white petals whirled around in the gentle breeze that punctuated the gorgeous summer's day.

"You do realise that this is where we first kissed?" Arial asked, the smile in her eyes flattering her pretty features.

"Yes," said Cinderella. "I remember it very well. I've replayed it in my mind many times since."

"Well," Arial said playfully. "I think it's only right that we do the same thing today."

"That's beautiful," said Cinderella. "I agree."

"For years to come," said Arial. "I want to walk in this garden with you as much as we possibly can. Enjoying the outdoors together, enjoying our safe, tranquil space, away from the craziness of the world. I think that's one of my favourite things about being with you; you make me feel at home, and at peace."

The two of them looked at each other compassionately. The feeling was mutual.

Holding each other as they rocked gently together against the warm breeze of the day, there was an energy between them that could be compared to nothing else. It was unique, and it was *theirs*. With that, they began to kiss. There were many memories to create, and they had found their happily ever after.

****